A SINFUL PROPOSITION

(The Sin Club Book 3)

RACHELLE CHASE

Printed in the United States of America

ISBN-10: 0-9864-2423-4
ISBN-13: 978-0-9864242-3-6

ACKNOWLEDGMENTS

Special thanks to my family, as always. I love you.

And, of course, a humongous thanks to my readers for reading my books—and making it all worthwhile.

A WORD FROM THE AUTHOR

This is a work of fiction, not a guide to real life. As such, my characters don't use condoms.
But real people should in real life.

Join the conversation at:
www.rachellechase.com/condom-conundrum-are-condoms-really-necessary-in-romance-novels/

1

"*Today* is the day to 'sin,'" Alyssa James said as she plopped down onto the lime green micro-suede chair in her best friend's office. She stared at Shannon, waiting for her response.

"You've got to stop listening to that garbage on the radio," Shannon said absently, not bothering to look up from whatever she was doing on her laptop.

"*The Sin Club* is not garbage. Dr. Love has successful sinners on his show every night. Today is my day."

"You've said that every day for the last 30 days."

"It's the power of positive thinking. I feel that *today* is going to be different."

Shannon shook her head. "How would you even know if you're sinning, Alyssa? You already break all the rules on your online blog."

Shannon had a point. Alyssa had started her blog, Sex in San Francisco, as a joke—she'd grabbed her camera and hit the streets of San Francisco, looking for interesting occurrences to write about. In a park in

Pacific Heights, she'd snapped a photo of two dogs—a perfectly coiffed Jack Russell terrier and a scruffy mongrel of unidentifiable heritage—in *flagrante delicto*. Afterward, she'd blogged about how opposites attract, even in the animal kingdom.

How was she to know that Fifi belonged to a prominent politician's wife? And how could she have guessed that the wife would call every radio and television station demanding that Fifi's photo be removed? Alyssa hadn't removed the photo, instead encouraging visitors to participate in the fracas online.

Sex in San Francisco was proof that *all* publicity was good publicity. Alyssa now dished the scoop on the private lives of San Francisco's rich and beautiful. But at a price. Hanging out in bushes and crashing parties left little time for a life of her own. So, while she did, indeed, "sin" for Sex in San Francisco, she had no time for personal sinning.

"I'm talking about sinning in my personal life."

"What personal life?"

"The personal life I'm about to have. I hired an assistant."

"That just means that you'll find more work for both of you to do."

While Alyssa didn't blame Shannon for her skepticism, a little best-friend humoring would've been nice. The negative energy rolling off of Shannon in waves was starting to put a dent in her conviction that today was *the* day.

She sighed. Loudly.

Shannon finally looked up and asked with resignation, "So what personal sin are you finally going to commit today?"

Alyssa grinned. "I'm glad you asked. I'm thinking

about sex. After all, shouldn't the blogger of Sex in San Francisco be having sex?"

"Umm-hmm." Shannon's gaze returned to her computer.

"Yeah, I know. I've always been a commitment gal—"

"An understatement," Shannon said. "Three years with Phil, four years with that loser from high school, four years—"

"Well, now I'm thinking, the heck with that. I can't afford the time for a relationship."

"Especially," Shannon muttered, "with the emotionally needy guys you get involved with."

Alyssa ignored that. "But I have time for a fling. If I'm willing to sin. That is, just go up to a hot guy and proposition him."

Shannon snorted. "Now, that I'd like to see. In fact, I'd pay to see that—you propositioning someone."

"Very funny." Alyssa decided to change the subject. "So how's business at The Perfect Date?"

"Slow. You know how tough startups are."

"Yeah."

"If I don't get a burst of business soon, I'm afraid . . ." Shannon sighed. After a minute, she beamed, instantly transformed into the poster child for positive thinking. "But I got a new client today." Once again, she tore her eyes away from her computer screen. "You won't believe who called me to hire a *corporate* escort!"

Alyssa smiled. Shannon always emphasized the word "corporate" lest anyone think she dealt in sexscorts—a term she coined for the less reputable escort services.

"Barney," said Alyssa.

"Barney Gaffney? Why would he need my services?"

"No. I meant Barney, from television. And I can think of one hundred reasons as to why he'd need your services. One, he's dull. Two, he lumbers around—"

Shannon sighed heavily.

Alyssa smiled. "Okay, okay. I'll be serious. Who?"

Before she could answer, the phone rang and Shannon answered. Nanoseconds later, she grinned. "Please send him in, Charlotte."

Shannon stood up.

Alyssa gathered her purse and prepared to stand.

"No. Don't go. I want you to see this."

Alyssa shrugged and settled back into her chair.

The elation in Shannon's face suddenly faded and she directed a stern look at Alyssa. "You *cannot* put this on your gossip blog."

Indignation rumbled in Alyssa's stomach. "I do not deal in gossip. I deal in facts and—"

"Alyssa!"

"Of course I won't. You know I never write about personal or confidential—"

The soft whoosh of the office door opening, coupled with the ass-kissing grin spreading across Shannon's face, stopped Alyssa in mid-protest. Alyssa turned toward the door, desperate to see who could bring such an abomination to the mouth of her no-nonsense friend.

"Mr. Brooks. Please come in," Shannon gushed behind her.

The Mr. Brooks—as in, Tony Alfonso Brooks . . . as in, owner of Flush, The Gilded Cage, Bubbles, and a dozen other upscale bars . . . as in the very single, very sexy, Antonio Banderas clone whose private life was a mystery.

And here she'd been given a glimpse into that mystery . . . That the most eligible man in The City apparently had to pay to get a date. Priceless. Glee bubbled up inside her. What a great story this would—

Damn. There was no story. She'd just promised Shannon she wouldn't write about him.

How could Shannon do this to me?

Just last week, Alyssa had written a piece speculating on the likelihood that Tony Brooks and supermodel-turned-restaurateur Chantelle Dubois had eloped to Sarlat, France.

Obviously that wasn't true, since he was standing in front of her. So putting Mr. Brooks within touching distance but saying she couldn't write about him was like . . . like . . . putting a fudge sundae in front of a child and saying, "don't eat it."

As Tony glided into the room in a navy Versace suit, Alyssa's racing heart, fluttery stomach, and rise in body temperature told her that he was like a fudge sundae in other ways—delicious, decadent, and deadly.

"Shannon, thanks for seeing me on such short notice." Smiling, he extended his hand to Shannon.

"My pleasure. Before we begin, let me introduce you to Alyssa James."

No, no. Don't introduce me.

". . . Alyssa, this is Mr. Tony Brooks."

Just this once, why hadn't Alyssa listened to her mother? When Alyssa was a teenager, her mom had always stressed to never leave the house without looking one's absolute best. Well, today Alyssa had left the house looking her absolute worst—no makeup, ponytail looped through the back of a "Just Do It" black Nike baseball cap, olive green cargo pants. The only item of clothing saving her from total fashion disaster was her fuchsia Bebe T-shirt.

Tony seemed to agree, for his eyes lingered on her breasts.

Alyssa blushed.

His gaze returned to her face. "She's not quite what I expected but . . . the long brown hair and doe-like eyes definitely work."

Alyssa's mouth dropped open.

Tony's gaze dropped to her mouth. "Nice, pouty lips. A little glossy stuff would help."

Glossy stuff? The nerve, utter gall. Why—

His gaze traveled lower. "Great breasts . . ."

Alyssa's face felt crimson. "How—"

"Kind of hard to make out the rest of her in those unattractive pants, but I'm guessing she's about a size eight?"

Once again, his eyes returned to her face. He raised a brow, as if expecting an answer.

I'm a size six. Alyssa's lips tightened.

His gaze returned to her lips.

Maybe he was imagining them coated in "glossy stuff." Or maybe he was imagining the feel of them against his, pressing and nibbling, while her hand caressed his Michelangelo-carved cheeks, before she trailed her fingers to his black, shoulder-length hair, freeing it from the band that held it, running her fingers—

No. That was her imagination, not his. Silly twit.

Her jaw clenched. "Would you like to see my

teeth, Mr. Brooks?"

He seemed to consider the question. "I hadn't thought about it, but it might be a good idea—"

"I am not a horse, Mr. Brooks, and I find your—"

Shannon's laugh had an edge of hysteria. "Don't you just love her sense of humor?"

His eyes narrowed, no longer seeming to assess horseflesh, instead searching for a hint of the sense of humor Shannon had promised.

Alyssa smiled, careful to hide all her teeth.

"Why, just before you arrived we were discussing how *today* was her day."

Alyssa looked at Shannon, whose smile was one step away from a grimace. *Don't fuck this up for me,* her look said.

Don't fuck what up? Alyssa shot back. *I don't know what the hell is going on here. One second I'm talking about* The Sin Club *and the next minute I'm being stripped and—*

Her words echoed in her mind: *Today is the day to "sin."* Shannon was trying to remind her of that.

Alyssa's eyes widened. She jerked her head in Tony's direction. "You want *me* to be his date?"

"You hadn't figured that out?" asked Tony.

"No. I'm not a—"

Tony grinned. "Then you're perfect." He turned back to Shannon. "I'll take her."

2

I'll take her.

Alyssa glared at Shannon. Shannon held her gaze for a second, then rounded her desk and walked toward Tony. She slipped her professional mask back into place.

"Mr. Brooks, maybe you ought to consider a couple of other candidates." She took his arm and drew him toward the outer office. "I've got some books with photos and bios."

"Shannon, I've made up my mind." He motioned behind him, in Alyssa's direction. "I want her."

"Okay, then I'll just have you fill out some paperwork." Shannon ushered him out of the office. At the door, she paused and looked back at Alyssa. *I'll be back,* she mouthed, then turned away.

Oh, yes, Shannon would definitely be back. There were a couple of little things they needed to discuss.

I'll take her.

Bartered for like a sack of flour, that's how those words had made her feel. Alyssa tucked a loose strand of hair behind her ear and watched Tony through the glass office door. So confident, so arrogant.

I'll take her.

So exciting.

Those words shouldn't thrill her, but they did. They ought to offend her. But now as she stared through the glass at the sexy man sitting there, talking with Shannon, she reconsidered.

"Maybe I'll take you," she whispered. On the plush beige carpet covering Shannon's office, or the outer office, or the elevator . . .

Sinful images flickered through her mind. Images of his finely tailored suit jacket lying crumpled at his feet. The white shirt unbuttoned to the waistband of his pants. A noticeable bulge decorating his perfectly pleated slacks . . .

And as Alyssa slides up to him, she's dressed only in his scarlet and black paisley tie, his eyes rove her body. No longer wearing the analytical gaze of an experienced horse trader, his eyes glisten with lust as he reaches for her, pulling her close, letting the friction of his shirt against her skin turn her nipples to hard pebbles, and the feel of his hard cock against her naked pussy—

"Stop looking at him like that," Shannon snapped, coming back into the office and checking that the glass door was locked.

Alyssa blinked.

She was no longer naked. Tony no longer had a hard-on.

She turned to Shannon. "Stop looking at him like what?"

"Like . . . you want to sin with him!"

"But I do want to sin with him."

"You can't."

Alyssa frowned. "What do you mean, I can't?

Didn't you just remind me that today was my day, in front of him?"

"Yes, and it is your day—to help me now and sin later. The Perfect Date does not employ prostitutes, call girls, or sexcorts. We are a 'corporate' escort service."

"Technically, I'm not an escort. So why can't I have sex with him?"

"Technically, you *will* be an escort. Alyssa, I could get my business license revoked, not to mention have some sort of criminal charges filed against me if the state found out my employees were having sex with clients." Shannon's voice was panicked.

"All right, all right," Alyssa muttered. "What else would I have to do? Not that I've agreed to do anything yet."

Shannon's smile was weak. "Oh, just be agreeable and friendly and . . . a perfect date."

"That's it?"

"Yeah, pretty much."

Alyssa tapped her finger against her chin. "And I can have sex with him after the date?"

"Yes."

Surely she could resist him for twenty-four hours.

Alyssa grinned. "I'll take him."

3

Alyssa stared out the window of Tony's Mercedes convertible, ignoring the landscape. Instead, her thoughts were on her dilemma. Apparently, resisting Tony was going to be harder than she'd thought.

When Shannon had told him that Alyssa would be his date, Tony had turned his megawatt smile on her—and her stomach had flopped and her panties had felt wet.

When he'd taken her arm to escort her out of the office, his firm grip had sent her mind back to the fantasy—making her imagine his fingertips on her naked flesh and his body heat as he'd reached around in front of her to open the door for her—she'd wanted to lean back, press herself against him, and make his cock as hard as she'd imagined.

I'll take her.

Well, she couldn't stop wanting to take *him*. In Shannon's office. In the elevator that had whisked them down to the garage. In the car that they were in right now.

Well, maybe not right now, since they were speeding down Highway 101 toward the coastal town of Mendocino at what had to be 120 miles per hour.

But she'd like to have him pull over to the side of the road, and then she'd lean over and trace his jaw with her fingertip.

"Do you know what I'm going to do to you?" she'd whisper throatily in his ear.

She'd run her hand down the front of his slacks, finding the zipper and pulling it down, before finding *him*.

She'd laugh sexily. "I see you do know what I'm going to do to you."

She'd take his cock in her hand.

He'd gasp.

She'd turn all the way toward him and climb over the gearshift, climb onto his lap and his hands would grip her ass, pulling her, guiding her—

". . . all right?"

Alyssa snapped her head from the pasture blurring in front of her eyes and looked at him. Loose strands of his hair danced in the breeze from the top-down convertible. She let her eyes travel over the chiseled jaw that she'd just touched in her mind.

He turned to look at her.

She blushed. "I'm sorry. My mind . . ." *was on straddling you, putting your cock inside me, and*— ". . . wandered."

"I asked if you were all right."

Get a grip, Alyssa.

Right. She was supposed to be a professional "corporate" escort. She was supposed to pay attention and string together coherent sentences.

Alyssa cleared her throat and summoned the

experienced escort from deep within. "Yes, I'm fine."

His long lean fingers—the same ones she'd imagined holding her ass—moved to the radio. "Would you like to listen to music?" he asked, pressing a button on the radio at the same time.

Whatever you like—that's what Shannon would tell her to say.

A replay of a prior *Sin Club* radio episode filled the air.

"Anything but that," Alyssa muttered.

"You don't like *The Sin Club?*"

No. Today she did not like Dr. Love. Yes, she was sinning because of him. But couldn't she have chosen a better guy to sin with? One who didn't view her as . . . hired help? One she hadn't just profiled on her Web site?

Whatever you like.

She made a sound that he could take either way.

Tony's tone was amused. "You must be the only woman in the nation who doesn't like the show."

And you're probably an expert on most of the women in the nation, aren't you?

". . . So, what was your sin, Sharice?" asked Dr. Love, his unique deep voice oozing sexiness from Tony's speakers.

"I was unhappy with the brothas I was meeting, so I decided to call Shawn, this man I'd met—a new experience for me," said a sultry feminine voice.

"Your first sin. Good. Go on."

"Only, I unknowingly misdialed. Jamal called me back, but I thought he was Shawn, and we made arrangements to meet for drinks. Shawn didn't show up, but I met Jamal, not knowing he was also Shawn . . ."

"Uh, Sharice? This is a bit hard to follow. What's your sin?"

"Oh. Right. My second sin was I had phone sex."

Dr. Love laughed. "You go, girl."

Tony laughed. "Now, *that's* a sin."

Alyssa inhaled sharply at Tony's words. The admiration in his tone indicated approval. Did he like phone sex? Now, there was an idea. Of calling him up and teasing him with some of the titillating thoughts running through her mind. Since phone sex wasn't exactly sex, maybe it wasn't banned in the "corporate" escort bylaws.

". . . and my last sin, well, I let go of my fear, and gave into a relationship."

Did every person who called in to Dr. Love have sins that led to a relationship? What about those who were looking for hot sex with a gorgeous, successful man who made your insides—

"Have you sinned, Alyssa?" asked Tony.

His words yanked her back to the present. "What?"

Tony grinned. "Too personal?"

That was an understatement. Nothing but sins had been running through her mind from the moment she'd met him.

"All right, I guess so. We'll start with something easier. Do you have a boyfriend?"

"Uh, no."

"I imagine being a Perfect Date keeps you pretty busy."

"Uh, no. I just started at The Perfect Date."

This time, his smile was sexy. "So I'm your first?"

Alyssa's stomach flipped over. "Yes."

His eyes took a quick tour of her body before he

returned his gaze to the road. "I'll do what I can to make your first time good."

Oh, God. He did not just say that.

Her mind instantly zoomed to their imaginary first time. Of her on top of him, looking down into those intense gray eyes glazed by the need she ignited in him. Her hips would move slowly on his cock as she stared into his eyes, watching the desire become need and—

And whatever you do, no sex, Alyssa, Shannon had said. . . . *if the state found out my employees were having sex with clients . . .*

Oh, God. How could Shannon say that?

Well, "the state" wasn't in the car with them right now. And she'd be willing to bet no ménage with state officials was being planned for them tonight.

Alyssa sighed, regretting that she had agreed to this "sin." No sex with the sexiest, wealthiest, most sought after man in the Bay Area. No inside scoop on the sexiest, wealthiest, most sought after man in the Bay Area for her avid readers.

How the hell was she going to avoid both of those no-nos? If a miracle occurred and she did, Shannon was going to owe her for the rest of their lives.

Alyssa stared at his profile, noticing that not only was his hair longer than any man's she'd ever been with, so were his eyelashes. If not for the masculine jawline, the slight bump in his nose that hinted at a long-ago break, he'd be almost perfect.

An almost perfect date.

Yeah, well, that was a first, too—being with a man who was prettier than she was. Not that she was Miss Universe or anything, but she could hold her own at Hooters. But, being with a man—

"Did Shannon tell you what you need to do?"

"Yes." *Whatever you like. And no sex.* Alyssa suppressed a sigh. "But it would be helpful to hear it from you."

He changed lanes and passed a slow-moving SUV before continuing. "I made an offer on a nightclub called Strands, but the owner, Giovanni Maffucci—"

"Giovanni Maffucci, the . . ." *sleaze bucket whom she'd written about on Sex in San Francisco?* ". . . guy who owns the string of strip clubs?"

Tony shot her an admiring glance.

Alyssa puffed up with pride—and lust—which instantly dissolved into apprehension. Were they going to meet Giovanni?

She couldn't meet Giovanni. He might recognize her. He—

Wait a minute. The odds of him recognizing her were right up there with Tony falling in love with her. There was no photo of her on her Web site. And she couldn't remember a photo of her ever being published. Plus, he wouldn't recognize her name, since she wrote her entries under the name of Erica Allen.

She was safe from love and discovery.

"Yes. Well, he's playing two ends against the middle. He's invited those who've made offers to his estate. This weekend it's my turn."

Tony's kissable lips twisted. "He wants to get to know us so he can choose the best man for Strands."

"You don't believe him?"

He shrugged. "It's not a question of belief. It's a question of business."

"I'm not sure I understand."

"Giovanni is choosing a buyer based on emotional

criteria." He turned from the road, his gray eyes burning Alyssa in their intensity.

Her breath froze in her chest.

"Business is about making the best deal. Emotion has no place in the transaction."

"Oh . . ."

He turned back to the road.

She let the breath leak from her lungs.

The steeliness underlying his tone implied that he was talking about more than this business deal—that there were other areas in his life where emotion didn't belong. Had some woman broken his heart?

Alyssa almost snorted at the thought. More likely he'd broken a string of hearts. All a woman had to do was look into those gray eyes that made her feel like the center of his universe, or see his sexy lips parted in a smile that melted the panties right off her hips and sent flutters—

". . . and just smile vacantly, stare adoringly at me, pay attention to my every word . . ."

The sudden awareness of his words pushed all thought of thongs and illicit flutters from her mind.

Did he just say what she thought he did?

"You want me to play a brainless . . . ditz?"

A frown marred his perfectly smooth brow. "Of course."

Of course?!

"Shannon said she'd tell you all this."

Oh, just be agreeable and friendly and . . . a perfect date, Shannon had said. No wonder the look on her face had been odd—a cross between indigestion and excess gas.

"She expressed it a tad differently."

"Is there a problem?" That steely, icy business

tone was back. The one that said there'd better not be a problem.

"No," she lied.

"Good." His frown disappeared. "Giovanni is a notorious male chauvinist. An intelligent date would convince him I was not the right man for Strands." The last sentence dripped with disdain, though from the date part or the being thought of as the wrong man, she couldn't tell.

"And Giovanni likes brunettes?"

Tony turned toward her. This time, his smile caused shivers to prickle her skin. "No. *I* like brunettes." His gaze dropped, lingering on her breasts, reminding her that he thought she had great breasts.

Her face heated. Her nipples tightened.

His smile seemed knowing as he turned back to the road.

"And do you like brainless women?" She was pleased to hear the amusement in her tone.

"No. Ditzes are not my type."

"Then what is your type?" Her voice sounded sultry, kind of like that woman—what was her name? Sharice?—on Dr. Love's show. A sinning voice.

Shannon would disapprove.

Tony's look said he approved. "I'm into women with brains."

"As long as they have great breasts," she quipped.

He shot another lingering look at hers. His smile was sly. "That does help . . ."

Alyssa's breasts tingled as if he'd reached over and touched them. She wished he *would* reach over and touch them, first slipping his hand under her shirt and . . .

She had to stop letting her thoughts drift down the road to sex—a road that had a huge barricade blocking all traffic for the duration of this trip.

Alyssa sighed.

They rode in silence for a couple miles. The covert glances she sent Tony's way showed him to be the picture of relaxation—his hand tapped the gearshift lightly and his head bobbed slightly, both keeping the beat to a Keith Urban song coming through the speakers. His gaze occasionally left the road to glance at the wildflowers starting to bloom along the side of the highway or a barn in the distance or . . . whatever.

Over on her side of the car, Alyssa's body felt as tense as an arched bow. Tony's body heat was like an invisible caress, enveloping her, tickling her skin, and injecting an overdose of hormones into her veins. And his comments that hinted at the fact that he was attracted to her encouraged her fantasies to saturate her mind.

She frowned.

And just why was he insinuating that he found her attractive—well, at least certain parts of her?

He had stressed that her purpose here was business. If that was the case, wouldn't he have picked a woman who appealed to Giovanni Maffucci, a woman who didn't have to pretend to be a ditz?

That, coupled with his comments, proved that his "hints" were real. He must find her attractive. Despite her "unattractive pants." Despite—

Oh, no. She didn't have an adequate wardrobe for hobnobbing with big—sleazy?—dealmakers. Maybe she should ask if they could stop somewhere to pick up a couple of dresses and some shoes.

"Mr. Brooks—"

He waved a hand. "Don't call me Mr. Brooks. It's Tony—No . . ." He paused before continuing. "We need something more . . . intimate . . ." He snapped his fingers. "You'll be Lissy."

She was appalled. "Lissy?"

"And you'll call me Tonykins."

"Tonykins!"

Tonykins shot her a grin.

Lissy groaned.

What had she gotten herself into?

4

As Alyssa stared in horror at the clothing spread over the bed in the guest suite she and Tony would be sharing at Giovanni's estate, she began to understand exactly what she'd gotten herself into:

T-r-o-u-b-l-e.

She picked up one of the dresses Tony had bought for her. Holding the black material up to the light, she stretched it, hoping to make it expand.

She relaxed her grip.

The dress shrunk to its original Barbie-doll size.

"I can't wear this!"

Tony came up behind her. His suit jacket brushed her back as he reached forward, taking the dress from her.

His nearness called to her, making her want to forget the dress in front of her, forget about all types of clothing, instead stripping off their own clothing and adding it, one piece at a time, to those on the bed.

Tony flipped over the tag in the back of the garment. "Did I get you the wrong size?"

His breath caressed her ear.

She wanted to tilt her head to the side and move her ear to his lips.

His arm pressed against her shoulder.

She resisted the urge to run her fingers along his forearm, dipping her fingertips under his shirt cuff and teasing the sensitive skin at his wrist.

His chest touched her back.

One teeny tiny step backward and she'd feel his body pressed up against hers . . . A shimmy or two of her hips, and she might feel his cock harden against her ass . . . A 180-degree pivot would land her in his arms, pressed against his chest, chin length away from his kissable lips . . .

Alyssa forced thoughts of his nearness away and her attention went back to the dress in hand. "It's barely . . . there."

"Giovanni will like it." His tone was matter-of-fact.

Who cares?

"I like it." His tone was melted chocolate.

All righty, then. Now, I care. But still . . .

He lifted the dress by the straps. "Here. You hold it."

She took it from him.

"Now, place it against you."

Alyssa held it against her, pinning it to her shoulders with her fingertips.

"I think it'll fit you perfectly . . . here." Tony stretched the dress across her chest.

His chest pressed against her back.

Alyssa gasped.

Stretching the material and moving his hands down, his fingers grazed the outside of her breasts and wound around to her stomach.

"And it'll fit you perfectly here." His palms flattened against her stomach, pressing lightly.

His groin grazed her ass, just enough to let her know that his cock was hard, just enough to drive her wild with the desire to grind her hips against him.

And whatever you do, no sex, Alyssa.

She really did not think she was going to be able to keep that promise. Maybe Shannon would accept a compromise: Alyssa would have sex with Tony but she wouldn't write about him.

"Would you wear it for me?"

Oh, God. Right now, she felt like she would do anything for him. As long as it resulted in what her body was craving right this second. The feel of him inside her, her legs wrapped around his waist, her arms around his neck, his mouth suckling her nipples, while her hips pumped and his hips thrust . . .

Alyssa jerked away, desperate to break the pull of his body, his ability to send her into a sexual daze. She took a step toward safety—that is three steps forward and out of reach of his invisible caress—so that she could think.

When she turned around, Tony had moved and was leaning against the door frame of the open closet door. Arms crossed, legs crossed, amused expression, and . . . aroused.

"Okay. I'll wear the dress. But, that bed . . . "

Her gaze went to the king-size bed. This time, she ignored the clothing strewn across it, instead taking in the silk, brocade pillows of every size that were piled high on the mattress, while filmy gold material hung from the sides of the canopy, tied back with thick rope.

Rope.

That sent a whole other set of images through her mind, of Tony bound and helpless, waiting for her touch, straining forward for more as she teased and taunted him with her body and her tongue, stroking his cock just enough to keep him hot and ready, but making him wait. Making him moan—

". . . It's fit for a sultan," she finished.

"Would you like me to ask for different bedding?"

"No." Her gaze darted back to him.

His gaze was teasing.

"Tony, I cannot sleep with you in that bed."

"Then you don't have to *sleep* with me in that bed."

She nodded. "Good. Then I think we should ask for a roll-away . . ." Her voice trailed off as she realized he'd meant those words an entirely different way.

Amusement had fled from his face. His gaze was erotically serious.

Her heart pummeled her ribs.

"Tony, I'll be honest. I really want to have sex with you—"

"Great."

He walked toward her.

She put a hand out in front of her. Her hand trembled.

"I didn't mean now." Her voice shook.

He stopped in front of her and placed a hand at the back of her neck, his thumb under her chin, tilting her head up. His thumb caressed her chin. "Tonight then."

He lowered his head.

She turned her head.

His lips grazed her jaw.

"Oh!"

His mouth nibbled, working its way back to her mouth.

"We both signed a contract agreeing to no sex so if you are still interested in me after this 'date,' then I would like to have sex with you." The words came out in a rush—breathless and garbled—because of the blood pounding in her head, the shakiness invading her body, and the weakness that had seeped into her muscles, making it require all her concentration to stand upright and not press herself forward and send Tony backward, until he was sprawled under her on the bed.

There. She'd done it. Propositioned a hot guy for sex.

She'd sinned, just as she promised. And in a way that honored her agreement with Shannon.

She felt proud.

Well, she would've felt proud if Tony's lips hadn't moved to the corner of her mouth, hovering, waiting.

"Deal," he said. His breath teased her. "Seal it with a kiss."

Before she could think about the wisdom of solidifying a deal with a kiss, his mouth captured hers. His mouth moved slowly and thoroughly over hers, persuading a response from her.

His hand caressed her neck. His lips caressed her lips.

Alyssa surrendered, gave in to the pull.

She kissed him back. She slipped her hands underneath his suit jacket, slid them up his back, and pulled him closer, needing to feel her chest pressed against his.

He deepened the kiss, his lips no longer

persuading, but seducing. His tongue no longer exploring, but plundering.

Alyssa moaned into his mouth.

He used the moan against her, taking it as a sign of permission. His hand slipped from her neck to her waist, pulling her hips against his, making her feel him, his need.

His thumbs caressed the skin under the hem of her T-shirt.

The voice of reason told her that the kiss was moving beyond the equivalent of a handshake, veering into a zone that was wild and carnal.

Stop, the little voice whispered in her head.

"You taste good," Tony whispered against her lips.

She liked Tony's whisper better than the voice in her head.

His mouth moved from hers, nibbling its way across her jaw, to her ear. His hands slipped farther under her T-shirt, moving up her sides, his thumbs brushing the underside of her breasts.

Alyssa moaned again.

"You feel so good," he said.

Alyssa liked this whisper the best.

She moved her hands from his back to his front, sliding them up his chest, to his neck. She removed the band from his hair, and tangled her hands in it, letting the silky strands caress her fingers.

Stretching upward and winding her hands around his neck, she pressed the full length of her body against him.

This time, he moaned.

His mouth moved to her neck. His hands went back to her waist, his grip firm as he pulled her toward him, rubbing his hips against hers, his cock kissing her pussy.

"Oh, yes," she breathed, pressing her hips forward, tilting them upward, then downward.

The air hissed from him. His grip tightened, holding her still.

"If you want to keep our deal," he rasped against her neck, "then you have about five seconds to move away from me."

Alyssa opened her eyes, becoming aware of her mouth against Tony's neck, her hands fisted in his hair, her breasts flattened against his chest, her hips pressed as close as she could get them to his.

She was even standing on tiptoe for better access.

So much for showing restraint. It was pretty bad when the guy had to tell you to stop. Alyssa's face felt warm.

She slid her body down his.

He cursed, his hands tightening on her waist.

"Oh. Right. The deal." She took a deep breath. It was shaky. Staring at his neck, she straightened the collar that she had wrinkled. Probably when she had clutched it in her hands to pull him down to her. My God, he must think she was . . . desperate.

She was desperate. For his touch. For his taste.

"Sorry. I kind of forgot about the deal for a minute. Despite my actions, I do want to stick to it. I—"

"Two seconds." His voice was strained.

"Oh." Alyssa pulled back, out of his arms. "Well, then. I'll just take this dress and go get ready."

She yanked the dress from the floor, unaware that it had fallen, and scampered past him, heading for the bathroom.

"Alyssa."

She paused and turned, forcing herself to look at him.

His hair hung to his shoulders, mussed as if a woman had ran her hands through it. His lips looked darker, as if a woman had kissed him repeatedly, giving him all the passion that had lain sleeping inside of her—passion that she hadn't thought about in a while. His clothing looked rumpled, as if a woman had pulled and tugged at it, desperate to get him naked and feel his flesh against hers.

Alyssa had done all of that—and wanted to do more.

She met his gaze.

His eyes were narrowed. "I only stopped because of you. Your job. I can't promise to next time."

With that, he turned and exited the bedroom.

5

Tony stood in front of the bar in Giovanni's home office, watching the man's lips move, but paying little attention. Instead, he was thinking of Alyssa's lips. How they'd parted almost instantly under his, just as eager to let him explore as he'd been to explore. How soft and smooth they'd been, moving in sync with his, giving one minute, demanding the next.

And her body, pressed against his, urging him to take her . . .

His cock stirred.

He'd wanted to fuck her. He couldn't remember wanting a woman so badly before.

As such, his parting words had been a half-lie. True, he couldn't promise that he'd stop next time. But the real truth was, he wasn't even going to try.

In a way, it was her fault—if she hadn't given him such a passionate response to his kiss, he'd let her hide behind that contract. But now . . . Hell, there was no way he was turning down the opportunity to see all that passion unleashed.

If only he didn't have this business with Giovanni to attend to.

Another first, when had some woman been more interesting than business? That thought caused him to frown. He pushed it from his mind and forced himself to pay attention to Giovanni.

". . . which is why Strands holds a special place in my heart . . ." said Giovanni.

Bullshit, thought Tony. Giovanni Maffucci's ego resided where his heart should've been.

". . . so I want a buyer willing to carry on the tradition . . ."

Which really meant he wanted a sucker to keep the club as is, which included preservation of the Maffucci shrine—complete with a wax figure of Giovanni behind glass—smack dab in the entrance to the club.

When Strands was his, Tony was considering having a bonfire at the grand opening, letting guests feed items of memorabilia into the flames.

Personally, Tony didn't like Giovanni. Giovanni screwed employees—literally and figuratively—implemented poor customer service, skimmed money by inflating expenses, and never reinvested the profits to improve the business. And those were his better qualities. It was a wonder that Strands was still showing a profit.

Profit was all that Tony cared about. Giovanni's sleaze factor was his own problem. Business was business.

As Giovanni gazed out the window toward the pool and droned on with feigned nostalgia, Tony's mind drifted back to Alyssa—correction: Lissy.

He smiled at the memory of her horrified

expression when he'd come up with their nicknames. And her near panic when she saw the clothes he'd bought for her to wear. That had been a switch—most of the women he knew would've hid their distaste, so intent on becoming the first Mrs. Brooks, no attire would have been unacceptable. Of course, Alyssa wasn't campaigning for a permanent position in his life.

Maybe that was her appeal. Well, that and the fact that she was a far cry from his usual dates—women who were artificially perfected, salon-pampered, botox-enhanced, and breast-augmented. Not that they were his type, either. They just seemed to be the ones he met in the entertainment business. The plastic women, who strove so hard for perfection, that they were almost untouchable—physically and emotionally.

The emotional part didn't bother him, as he had no desire—or time—for emotional involvement. But the physical part eventually became a showstopper. Perfection didn't mix well with sex that was hot, sweaty, and messy.

But hot, sweaty, and messy sex seemed like it would mix well with Lissy.

Because she oozed naturalness. Sun-kissed hair that he could weave his hands through. Smooth, makeup-free skin he could touch and nibble. Round, plump, real breasts that would fill his hands, that he could cover with licks and kisses, that he could caress and squeeze, sending lust crashing through both of them.

And those rosy, pouty lips. God, one quick taste of them had him fantasizing about feeling them on his skin, moving from his mouth and down his neck, her tongue swirling against his flesh, as she moved lower. To his chest, over his stomach . . .

His pants felt tight.

And, what surprised him was that he actually enjoyed talking to her. Not that they'd done more than sparred about this silly date-for-hire situation. But she'd made it . . . enjoyable.

Now, there was a word that hadn't been used in a sentence with his name in it for a very long time. No time. Business took up most of his time and, while he enjoyed it, it was a different type of enjoyment. Not that he was complaining. He hadn't even given it much thought until now.

Until Alyssa.

But of course, that was what she did for a living— making men feel at ease, making sure they enjoyed their . . ."date." He smiled. Scratch the word "men" and make it "man." He was her first. She was making sure that he enjoyed his date.

His smile faded and he frowned.

Is that what she'd been doing upstairs, pretending so that his "date" would be enjoyable?

No, she couldn't be. She'd have to be one hell of an actress—

A movement in the hallway outside the door drew his gaze. Unaware that she was being observed, Alyssa chewed her lower lip as she pulled—or tried to pull—the dress down to cover more of her thighs. She looked down the front of her dress and pulled up, attempting to cover her chest, but only succeeding in shortening its length.

Tony's cock lengthened.

Alyssa sighed, repeated the pulling-over-the-hip action, then cupped her breasts—

Tony swallowed. Hard.

—and pushed upward, then adjusted the drape of the slinky material. She took a deep breath that, to his cock's delight, pushed the fleshy globes tight against the fabric, revealing the slight outline of her nipples.

Feeling as if all the oxygen had been sucked from the room, Tony gulped in air.

Alyssa looked up. Surprise flitted across her face.

Tony smiled—what he hoped was a casual, hey-baby-you-look-good smile, not the leering, I'll-give-anything-to-be-inside-you smile he was feeling.

Alyssa blushed. Squaring her shoulders, she took another deep breath.

Like a trained lab rat, Tony's eyes once again dropped to her chest, obsessed by the nipples he suddenly prayed would pop out of the dress. When she exhaled, his gaze returned to her face.

She smiled. A sultry I'll-do-anything-to-be-with-you smile.

Stunned, the breath caught in his chest.

He watched her take small, bouncy steps into the room, her eyes never leaving his, the smile never leaving her face.

"Tonykins," she squealed.

He felt his mouth drop open.

"There you are. I thought I'd never find you. I got lost coming down the stairs, and there were all these hallways and doors . . ." She giggled and jiggled up to him. "But now I'm . . . here." She stood on tiptoe, her breasts pressing into his forearm.

Heat rushed to his groin.

He'd barely remembered to close his mouth when she pressed her lips against his. The softness of her lips, the minty scent of her toothpaste, coupled with her hot body pressed the length of his caused an instinctive craving to deepen the kiss. Just as he moved his lips against hers, she moved away.

"Oh . . . this handsome man must be Mr. Maffucci," she purred, sticking out a limp hand—when did she paint her nails hot pink? "So *very* nice to meet you."

Tony watched in amazement as Giovanni, who'd turned from the window when she'd flounced in, straightened and sucked in his gut. He took her hand in his, bringing it to his fleshy lips.

"You must be Alyssa. An unusual name but it sounds familiar." He paused for a minute, frowning.

Did Alyssa stiffen?

Giovanni's frown faded and he smiled—leered—and continued. "Tony neglected to mention how . . ." his gaze slithered over her body, lingering on her breasts. He licked his fleshy lips. ". . . charming you were."

Tony frowned.

Alyssa giggled. Again. "Oh, he always forgets to tell people that, don't you, baby?" She swatted his arm playfully.

Giovanni's gaze was still riveted to her breasts.

Tony's lips tightened.

He slid his arm around her waist and pulled her to him, pressing a light kiss on her forehead. "That's because I don't want to share you, Lissy." His voice had an edge he didn't mean it to.

Giovanni chuckled. "And well you shouldn't, my man."

Alyssa turned to Tony, her mouth a moue of surprise. "Baby, are you jealous?"

Tony felt his face grow warm. Of course he wasn't

jealous. He never—

She took his cheeks between her thumb and forefinger, pinching and jiggling them like one did an infant. "Oh, Tonykins," she said in baby talk, "you know I *wone-wee* want you."

Tony's face felt hot. No one had ever tweaked his cheeks and treated him like a baby, not even when he *was* a baby.

Giovanni laughed.

Alyssa smiled, slid her arm around his waist, pressed her body against his, and turned to Giovanni. "Were you boys discussing that business stuff?" She waved her hand dismissively before resting it on Tony's chest.

"Yes, as a matter of fact, we were," said Giovanni.

Alyssa fidgeted against him, her pussy rubbing against his thigh, while her fingers played with the button on his shirt. Tony gritted his teeth and placed his hand over hers, stopping their motion.

She looked up at him, pouting. "I hope you're done, Tonykins. You promised not to talk about boring stuff. You said we were going to have fun."

Keeping the lust careening through his body in check, he bent his knee slightly and rubbed his thigh lightly between her legs.

This time, her moue of surprise was real. As was her gasp.

He smiled down at her. "Baby, we are going to have fun. I promise."

"No time like the present," said Giovanni, oblivious to Tony's double entendre.

Alyssa wasn't. She blushed and quickly looked away, turning her attention to their host.

Satisfaction zinged through Tony. One point for

the home team. Finally.

"Tony, why don't you make us fresh drinks. And I'm sure Lissy is thirsty."

"Oh, yes." She nodded eagerly, her hair brushing her shoulders.

Giovanni looked just as eager as he took her hands and led her to the couch.

She sat.

Giovanni sat next to her. Too close.

Tony clenched his jaw, pivoted and went to the bar. "What would you like, Lissy?"

She waved at him dismissively, her rapt gaze upon Giovanni.

"The usual."

Barely paying attention to their conversation, he splashed whatever liquor his hands touched into a glass, then made a gin and tonic for Giovanni. In record time, he carried the glasses to the couch and sat next to Alyssa.

He put his arm around her shoulder and pulled her to him.

She took a sip, then coughed and sputtered, tears streaming down her face. "Wow," she said, glaring at him. "That's really good, Tonykins."

He grinned, feeling back in the game, and stroked her cheek with the back of his finger. "Only the best for you, baby."

"Thank you," she said sweetly. She stuck her tongue out at him before turning back to Giovanni. "I like a drink with a little . . . kick." She took another sip for show. Though her eyes watered, she didn't cough. She set the glass down. To Tony, it looked like with relief.

Tony sat back, suddenly enjoying himself.

"So tell me, Lissy, what do you do for a living?"

Tony took a sip, curious to hear what creative answer she was going to come up with.

"I'm a . . . gymnast."

Tony choked.

She turned to him, resting her hand on his thigh, drawing little circles with her forefinger against the fabric, faux concern plastered on her face. "Tonykins, are you okay?"

His cock woke up. He nodded, catching his breath.

She swung back around, before pressing hard against his leg, using his thigh for leverage to stand. "Wanna see some of my moves?"

"Yes!" said Giovanni.

"No!" said Tony.

Tony watched Alyssa bounce away from them. The dress hugged her thighs and cupped her ass. With each step, the exaggerated sway of her hips threatened to pull the tight material upward, giving a tantalizing glimpse of an ass cheek.

She stopped and turned toward them. She took a bow, revealing a cock-hardening amount of breast and cleavage.

Giovanni inhaled sharply.

Alyssa turned to the side and raised her hands over her head.

Tony sprang from the couch.

"I learned to do the splits when I was five—"

He reached her side and grabbed her arm. "You are not going to do the splits," he ground out.

He led her back to the couch and pulled her down, this time onto his lap where he could make sure she didn't go anywhere.

"I'm wearing a dress, silly—I wasn't going to do

the splits." Her tone was huffy. "I was going to do a handstand."

Giovanni laughed.

Alyssa pouted. "You didn't have to be such a pitty poo, Tonykins."

"I agree, pitty poo Tonykins," said Giovanni, chortling.

Alyssa squirmed and turned excitedly to Giovanni, "Your house is beautiful. Tell me all about it."

Giovanni puffed up and began telling about the rooms in loving detail. Since there was at least 6,000 square feet of living space, Tony figured the conversation was going to take a long time. Especially with Alyssa asking him questions and squealing and squirming with delight.

Alyssa wiggled again and Tony gritted his teeth, the hand that had been lightly stroking her shoulder, tightening, giving her the subtle hint to stop.

She stopped, thankfully getting the hint.

His head hurt. And he was so aroused, his balls hurt. This evening was not going as planned. He hadn't thought he'd have to sit around and watch Giovanni practically drool over Alyssa all night. Where the hell was his girlfriend?

Baby, are you jealous? Alyssa had chirped.

Hell, no. That was ridiculous. He just wanted this mind-numbing conversation to end.

Alyssa laughed at something Giovanni said and rubbed her ass against his crotch.

Desire stabbed his groin.

His head throbbed.

He leaned forward and whispered in her ear, "Do that one more time and I will send Giovanni on some errand and fuck you right here on this couch."

He kissed the back of her neck.

She stilled, not moving a muscle while Giovanni droned on. Tony forced his jaw to relax. Giovanni was getting on his last nerve. With every word that came out of his mouth, Tony's dislike for him grew. He was pompous, selfish, and an egomaniac. Tony'd much rather be sequestered with Alyssa upstairs, in bed—

Bed.

For the first time in over thirty minutes, Tony smiled. She'd called it a sultan's bed. Actually, it did resemble one. He wondered if there were any feathers in any of the drawers. If so, he'd lay Alyssa, completely naked, on the bed and make her lie still while he ran the feather down her body, over her neck, and across her shoulders, drawing circles on her breasts before lightly tickling her nipples. She'd gasp and arch, wanting more. Begging him to take her in his mouth, to—

"Shall we head to dinner?" asked Giovanni, interrupting Tony's fantasy.

"Yes!" he said.

"Yes, I'm famished!" said Alyssa.

Giovanni smiled for the hundredth time at Alyssa. "Good. I want you to meet Bimbi. I'm sure the two of you will have a lot to talk about."

Alyssa clapped her hands together lightly. "Oh, that sounds like fun."

As Giovanni led them from the room, Alyssa turned to Tony. Laughter sparkled in her eyes, her cheeks were flushed, and she looked thoroughly kissable.

He resisted the urge to lean down and make her face burn with a different kind of heat, to—

"Do you think 'Bimbi' stands for 'bimbo'?" she whispered.

"Speaking of bimbos, maybe you should tone down the ditzy act a bit."

"Oh, no," she said, surprise rippling through her tone. "Giovanni likes it. Your deal is in the bag. What—you don't think it's working?"

Hell, yeah, it was working. Too well. Giovanni looked about two steps away from making Alyssa part of the deal.

So what's the problem? If that's what it takes . . . Business is business, right?

6

Standing in the middle of the bathroom in Giovanni's pool house, Alyssa massaged her temples with the pads of her fingers. Her head was killing her. The strain of fawning all over Tony, of constantly sidling up to him, of feeling the muscles of his arm flex against her or the brush of his leg against her hip—

God, that was nothing compared to sitting on Tony's lap in Giovanni's office. *That* had been torture. Every time she'd moved, his cock was there, pressing against her ass, a constant reminder of what she wanted but couldn't have. And he kept moving, shifting his hips, pressing his cock closer, which caused her to move, to try to get comfortable, to try to move away.

Do that one more time and I will send Giovanni on some errand and fuck you right here on this couch.

His words, combined with the accompanying agonized growl, had almost brought her to orgasm. If he had kissed the back of her neck for just a second longer, she would've.

Then there was the agony of dinner, where Tony kept his hand on her thigh, massaging and caressing her under the table. What was up with that? Giovanni couldn't even see Tony's hand, so it couldn't have been for his sake. Unless Tony had wanted to keep Alyssa's face permanently flushed, thereby giving the appearance of continual arousal.

Appearances be damned. It was reality. Alyssa was aroused, more aroused than she could remember being in months.

Well, it didn't take much to top that record, for she hadn't been aroused *at all* in months.

Whatever.

Alyssa opened her eyes and walked to the sink. She stared at her face in the mirror. It was still flushed, still mirroring her lust.

She turned on the cold water, cupped her hands under the stream, and splashed water on her face. Again and again, then used the fluffy white hand towel to pat her skin dry.

She didn't feel any better. She still felt tense and her head still ached.

The constant state of arousal was the cause of her tension while the strain of being bubbly and perky and clueless had given her a headache. Or maybe it was the other way around. Or maybe both were caused by horniness.

Oh, what did it matter? What mattered was that her body and her mind were both tied in knots and she was strung as taut as a rubber band.

The next time she heard another dumb blonde joke, she was going to feel outrage because those who fit the cliché deserved respect. Being ditzy was damn hard work.

Speaking of work, it was time she got back to it.

Alyssa turned to the floor-length mirror on the door for one last look at the bathing suit Tony had bought for her. Eighty percent of her breasts spilled out of the miniscule triangles designed to cover little more than her nipples. And the bikini bottom . . . well, if she hadn't had a Brazilian wax done two days ago, things could've been quite ugly. Literally. That triangle that covered her pussy was only slightly wider and longer than the ones that failed to cover her chest.

She sighed.

Surely, being dressed like a stripper must be against some rule in Shannon's "corporate" escort handbook.

She wouldn't have thought it possible for the leopard skin patterned bathing suit to look sluttier on than it had spread across the bed.

Bed.

As in, the piece of furniture that she and Tony would find themselves lying atop in a handful of hours.

God.

How was she going to get through the night without . . . sinning—which would land her both in heaven, because of the heights to which Tony took her body, and in breach of contract, because she'd signed away the right for Tony to take her to heaven.

It made her head spin.

Letting out another deep sigh, Alyssa reached for the filmy wrap and tied it around her hips. Despite its see-through nature, she felt less naked. With one last look, she exited the bathroom, returned to the torchlit pool, and—

Stopped dead in her tracks.

Hyperventilation was added as ailment number five to her current list, preceded only by number four, want; number three, desire; number two, need; and number one, lust.

The source of ailment numbers one through five reclined on a lounge chair, clad only in a Speedo-type bathing suit. Unable to stop herself, Alyssa let her gaze wander hungrily over Tony's tanned legs, lingering on his muscular thighs and the muscle-of-choice, hidden behind the black Lycra, before moving higher over his toned abs and honed pecs.

God, how could it be possible for a man to *be* mouth-watering?

Struggling to mask her thoughts, she raised her gaze to his face only to discover that Tony had been taking a journey of his own. His gaze roved her body, lingering on the same spots that'd intrigued her when exploring his body. His eyes stroked her legs . . . caressed her thighs . . . penetrated the sheerness of her wrap and stroked her pussy, generating heat . . . circled her waist like a lasso, pulling her toward him . . . swept across her breasts, making her nipples peak and strain toward him . . . and finally, landed on her face.

His eyes smoldered.

"Alyssa, come join us," said Giovanni.

Her gaze flickered to him, taking note of Bimbi sprawled on a chair pulled close to his, her bathing suit equally as nonexistent as Alyssa's.

"Lissy, come join *me*," Tony said, drawing her attention back to him. His voice seduced, tangling with the invisible rope still looped around her waist, pulling her toward him.

Tony patted his chair.

Her gaze dropped to the spot he indicated, directly in front of his hips, before zooming in on the bulge in his trunks that hadn't been there seconds before.

If she sat in front of him, she'd feel his cock against her ass—again—and she'd lose the remnants of pride that she was hanging onto with her pinky and turn into him and kiss the lips that she'd been fantasizing about all evening, and roll on top of him, grinding her hips against his, desperate to feel him inside her.

Right in front of Bimbi and Giovanni.

Not that Giovanni would mind. He'd probably whip out his camcorder and film it for one of his "gentlemen's" clubs.

She shuddered. The night had shown her that Giovanni was a bigger sleaze than she'd imagined. Thank God Bimbi had arrived to take Giovanni's attention off Alyssa.

Or maybe she wasn't thankful. Because dealing with her revulsion to Giovanni was a thousand times easier than dealing with her attraction to Tony.

Nope. There was no way she was going over there to Tony's cock—er, chair. Just as there was no way she was going to be able to keep her no-sex promise to Shannon.

But she should at least give it one last try, shouldn't she?

Her panicked gaze returned to Tony's. His eyes were hooded, his lips curled in a slight smile that said he could see the battle going on inside her. He picked up a drink from the table beside the chair and held it out to her while, once again, patting the place in front of him with the other.

Getting drunk was the last thing she needed. What she needed was strength.

She giggled. "I want to swim first, Tonykins." Her giggle sounded like a cackle. Her voice sounded shrill. But she didn't care. Turning, she stripped off her wrap and dove into the pool.

He body sliced through the water. The water closed over her head, blocking out all sound, preventing her from hearing any response Tony might've made. Facedown, coming up for air every fifth or sixth stroke, she made her way to one end of the pool, turned, and swam to the opposite end. Once . . . twice . . . by the third time, she felt sufficiently winded and decided to slow down. When she reached the deep end, she grabbed hold of the edge and came to a sputtering stop.

"We thought maybe you were training for the Olympics," said Giovanni with a laugh from the poolside behind her.

She forced another giggle, unable to think of a brainless rejoinder, and wiped the water out of her eyes with one hand.

She'd hoped that the laps would help her work off some of her sexual tension, which still buzzed through her.

A loud splash, followed by the sound of strokes, caused her to turn her head in time to see Tony's body cut gracefully through the water, heading in the opposite direction.

Alyssa turned her body around so that her shoulder blades rested against the edge of the pool, stretching her arms along the ledge to hold herself afloat. She watched Tony turn, push off against the side of the pool and glide almost soundlessly toward her.

His muscles rippled with each stroke.

Her body throbbed with each stroke.

He stopped in front of her, treading water. His hair had come loose from the band holding it back and it hung in his face, covering his eyes. He ducked underwater, held his head back, and once again bobbed to the surface.

"Hi," he said, unsmiling.

"Hi," she said, breathless. Though more from his nearness than from the half dozen laps she'd just rushed through.

"You weren't thirsty, I take it."

"Thirsty?"

"The drink."

"Oh . . ." Her mind flashed back on the delicious visual—his hard cock straining against the tight material—that had sent her scurrying to the pool. *No, I was—am—hungry. Starving for a taste of you.* "No . . . I . . . You . . . "

He was too close. His breath blew all thoughts out of her mind, while flooding her body with need—the need to press closer.

She pressed her body back against the tiled wall.

He stopped treading water and kept himself afloat by holding on to the ledge on either side of her head. He dipped a leg between hers, his knee brushing her inner thigh. Alyssa clasped her legs together, preventing his leg from going higher.

She gasped. "Tony, this is not supposed to happen." She kept her voice low so Giovanni and Bimbi couldn't hear. Not that they could anyway, given they were at least thirty feet away.

"You're a beautiful woman. I'm a mere man."

Oh, God. A flesh-and-blood Roman god had just called her beautiful.

Her heart melted, her lips curved into a smile.

"What did you expect, coming out here almost naked?"

Her smile evaporated. "You bought this suit!"

"Doesn't change the fact that you're nearly naked." His fingertips caressed the sensitive skin of her inner arm.

His leg moved upward, despite the feeble attempt of her thighs to stop him, and nestled against her crotch. "The faint outline of your pussy lips made my cock hard."

She exhaled noisily.

He slid his hand fractionally and his fingers brushed the sides of her breasts.

She inhaled sharply.

He leaned forward, and spoke near her ear. "I could see your nipples harden when you saw my cock." His tongue flicked her earlobe. "You've been teasing me all night, Alyssa."

"You wanted me to tease you." Her voice cracked.

"I wanted you to adore me."

"How can I adore you without teasing you?"

"You should've asked that question a lot earlier."

No sex. No sex. No sex.

"Tony." Her voice pleaded. "I was just trying to do my job."

"You excel at your job. Your giggle reminded me of the sound a woman makes during sex. When she's being pleasured beyond her wildest dreams."

Oh, man, she wanted to be pleasured beyond her wettest, wildest, most graphic dreams.

"And your brainless act had Giovanni panting after you . . ." He nibbled her earlobe.

She shivered.

"I was jealous."

She gasped. "You were?"

His mouth moved to the corner of hers. His chest rubbed against hers. "I really would have fucked you there. You know that, don't you?"

"N-no."

"Do you know I'm going to fuck you now?"

His words made her lightheaded, as the blood rushed from her head and swelled her pussy lips. Desperation caused her to try a different approach. "But you don't like brainless women!"

"You've taught me to appreciate their appeal."

"But The Perfect Date code of ethics . . ." Her ace card. Her only hope of stopping him. "I signed it. Sex could cost me my job." Oh. Right. She didn't care if she had a job. "I mean, it could cost Shannon her business."

"I won't tell if you don't." His voice was like honey. His tongue traced her lips. "Kiss me, Alyssa."

She parted her lips to say . . . Yes . . . No . . . Ah, hell, she didn't know what she'd been going to say.

He bit her lip lightly. His thigh brushed against her thigh. Sensation pummeled her body.

She groaned.

"Alyssa."

"Yes?" she asked, not sure if she said the word out loud.

His tongue dipped between her lips. "Kiss me. Like you did before."

Oh, God, yes, kiss him, Alyssa!

Sorry, Shannon. I tried.

Alyssa moaned softly—a moan of surrender—and slanted her head. She moved her lips over his, sneaking her tongue inside his mouth, stealing a taste of rum mixed with need, lust mixed with man. She pressed forward, forcing the kiss deeper, demanding his passion.

A groan rumbled beneath his ribs. Pressing forward, he satisfied her demand, meeting her tongue thrust for thrust, taste for taste. Giving her his passion, while taking hers.

She wanted more than a kiss. More than the tease of his body brushing hers, the water trying to separate them.

Alyssa slid her foot up his leg.

His gasp filled her mouth.

She slid her foot down his leg.

He pressed his hips forward.

Her gasp filled his mouth.

"Wrap your legs around me." Pain underlined his words.

Sharing his pain, Alyssa wrapped her legs around his hips—and nearly fainted. His cock grazed her pussy, so close, so potent, despite the layers of stretchy fabric separating them.

She tightened her legs, pulling him closer. She removed her arms from the ledge and wrapped them around his neck. Her chest flattened against his, her pussy rubbed against his cock.

Tony moaned softly.

Giovanni yelled from the poolside, "Get a hotel room."

Bimbi tittered.

Alyssa opened her eyes, yanked from the world of the senses. Lust warred with . . . embarrassment.

Tony's cock pulsed against her lower lips.

Her nipples throbbed against his chest.

God, if Giovanni hadn't interrupted them, she would've fucked Tony right in front of his eyes. And what made things even worse was the fact that the lust still raging through her veins made her want to fuck Tony, regardless of who might be watching.

"We're thinking about it," said Tony, not taking his eyes off of her.

Giovanni laughed.

Tony didn't.

Alyssa slid her legs down Tony's body, intending to move away.

"Don't move," Tony said, removing one hand from the ledge to grab her leg and stop its slide.

"Tony, I don't think we—"

"Don't think." His head dropped to her neck, suckling. His fingers glided to her inner thigh, and slid underneath her suit, seeking . . .

"Oh—" she breathed.

. . . finding . . .

She gripped his neck, clutching him as if he were a lifesaver. Which, maybe he was, since he was now the only thing keeping her afloat.

His finger sped against her clit, making the little nub as rigid as the cock she felt through his trunks, which was caressing her thigh.

She struggled to remain still, for if she didn't grind her hips in time to his finger, urging him faster and harder, no one would know that Tony was finger banging her in the water, that she was two seconds from coming, that—

"Touch me," he rasped in her ear.

Still dazed by Tony's strokes, she removed one

arm from his neck, trailing it down his body, to his trunks. She slipped her hand inside, brushing the crinkly hair with her fingertips as they made their way to his cock.

Tony nipped her neck with his teeth.

His finger sped up, sending her higher.

She found her rhythm, circling his hardness, stroking his cock.

"Put me inside you."

Sanity made a brief appearance. "Not here. They'll know."

"You think they don't already know?"

His finger slipped into her pussy, then moved back to her clit. Pussy . . . clit . . . pussy . . . clit.

"You think they care? They've got business of their own."

Tony's back was to the poolside couple but Alyssa's wasn't. She raised her eyes and looked.

"Do you care, Alyssa? Are you going to tell me to stop?"

Her eyes fluttered closed, his words making her dizzy, while his finger made her body shake.

"No . . . "

"No, what?"

She opened her eyes, fighting Tony's spell for the briefest of seconds. She needed to know . . .

Sure enough, Giovanni and Bimbi weren't paying attention to her and Tony. In fact, they were about to get their own little orgy started, judging by the lip-lock Bimbi had him in.

Not that it mattered anymore. "No, I don't care."

Tony's probing fingers jerked her attention back to him.

"No, I don't want you to stop."

Her nails dug into his shoulders as the tension within her pooled in her pussy, swirling and roiling and . . .

She tried to hold back.

It was too much to hold back.

All the teasing and taunting, touching and caressing, had taken its toll. Tony's touch released the chaos churning inside her, causing it to explode outward, causing her body to tremble and quiver.

She managed to hold back the scream that lodged in her throat.

She managed to hold onto Tony, to not become the first woman to drown while coming.

God, that was great. Most probably the best—

"Alyssa?"

Alyssa blinked, coming back to reality for the second time in two minutes. She focused on Tony, noting the agonized expression on his face.

"Put me inside you."

Oh. Right. His needs. Give a girl a mind-blowing orgasm and, well, there goes her mind.

She lifted her legs higher, wrapping them around his hips, and positioned his cock near her pussy.

His fingers pulled her bikini bottoms to the side.

She put him at her entrance.

He jerked, straining to get closer.

And just like that, his cock turned his need into hers. Digging the heels of her feet into his ass, she pulled her hips forward slightly, letting him in an inch.

He cursed.

She gasped and buried him inside her another inch.

His hand left her, joining his other hand on the ledge. He tried to pump his hips forward, but had nothing to ground his legs against, so her back touched the edge of the pool, before the water carried them a few inches away.

Wow. Tony was helpless. While he had nothing to use as leverage and had to keep both hands—or at least one—on the ledge to keep them from drowning, her hands and legs were free. He was dependent on her for his satisfaction.

How cool was that?

This realization ratcheted her arousal up another ten degrees.

"Tony?"

"What."

Gee, that sure sounded painful.

"You want to be inside me . . . like . . . this . . .?" Using her heels, Alyssa pulled her hips all the way forward. A moan slipped from her throat.

"Oh, God." The words were a tortured moan from his throat.

Alyssa struggled to keep her desire in check, to focus on him. She clutched his shoulder with one hand to keep herself anchored, then grabbed his hip with the other. Pushing with the hand on his hip, she propelled her hips backward, away from him.

His cock slid halfway out of her pussy.

Pulling with her hand and her legs, still wrapped around his hips, she drew his cock back in her pussy.

"Is this what you had in mind, Tony?"

"Yes!"

She pushed him out of her, then pulled him back in.

"Faster."

She went faster. The water churned around them, disturbed by her actions, splashing up, getting in her eyes.

She closed her eyes, the turbulence in the water matching the turbulence inside her.

They made no effort to be quiet.

He called her name.

She cried out.

His breathing was ragged.

Her breathing was loud.

She was on the edge, the point where every nerve and cell seemed to be as one, motionless and waiting for the sensation roiling through her body to explode and send her insides into a flurry of motion.

All activity beyond what was being done to her body ceased to have meaning. At this moment, Tony's cock stroking her pussy was the only thing that mattered to her.

He grunted. He bit her shoulder. He moaned her name.

All of which broke the dam within her body, releasing the need struggling to get free.

Alyssa let go of Tony's hip and clutched his neck with both hands, holding on tight, pressing him as close as possible to her, needing to feel his spasms both inside and against her body.

Tony buried his head in the curve of her neck as his body surrendered to his release.

Alyssa listened to his breathing and the silence around them. Giovanni and Bimbi had left. The water was still.

Alyssa relaxed.

Once his body felt relaxed, she unwound her arms from Tony's neck and separated their bodies while simultaneously reaching behind her for the ledge.

She kissed his forehead.

He kissed her lips.

Inching to her right, Tony flattened his palms against the ledge and used his arms to push. He propelled his torso out of the water, then threw his leg onto the side of the pool, and stood.

Turning, he reached down, took Alyssa's hand, and pulled her out of the water.

Still holding onto her, he led her to the lounge chair and picked up her wrap and two towels. He wrapped one around her and tucked the other over his hips.

This time, he kissed her on her forehead and said, "Come on."

"Where are we going?"

He grinned and winked at her. "To bed."

7

Standing in front of the bed, Alyssa toweled her hair dry. Her skin felt clean. Her body felt energized—from the shower, certainly. From the knowledge of what was in store for her, most definitely.

The sound of drawers opening and closing drew her gaze to Tony.

"What are you looking for?"

He turned from the nightstand and grinned at her.

"Feathers."

"Feathers?"

"Yeah. While you were giving me that lap dance in Giovanni's office, I fantasized about spreading you naked on the bed, stroking your body with feathers, teasing you—"

Her body hummed from the visual. "Let me help you look." Her voice was a croak.

Tony laughed.

Both were disappointed when every drawer had been opened and every corner had been searched. No feathers.

Alyssa walked over to the bed, going to one set of curtains then the other, removing the ropes.

Ropes in hand, she walked over to Tony, who stood at the foot of the bed. "Great minds think alike," she said, rubbing the rope along his arms.

"How's that?"

"Well, while you were imaging feather torture, I was imagining tying you up with this rope and teasing you like this . . ." She ran her tongue over his chest, ending with his nipples.

They hardened.

". . . And this . . ." She wrapped her hand around his cock.

His cock hardened.

Tony wrapped his hands around her hand. "I don't do ropes." His voice was hoarse.

Her voice teased. "Is the mighty Tony Brooks afraid of a little brainless gal like me?"

"Yes," he said. He took her hands in his and forced her backward until her legs butted up against the bed. Slipping the rope from her hands, he pushed her.

She toppled onto the bed.

Tony climbed on top of her, straddling her hips. "Plus, it's my turn."

"Your turn for what?"

"To have you helpless. Like you had me in the pool."

He pulled her hand toward the headboard.

She pulled her hand back. "But you could've gotten away if you'd wanted."

"The knots will be loose so you can slip out of them if you want. But I hope you won't."

Tony tied one arm, then the next.

Alyssa shivered. "I feel silly. Like a pig ready for roasting." Her laugh was nervous.

Tony parted the towel and ran his hands over her—down her breasts, stomach, hips and back up.

The touch stoked a familiar fire.

"You don't look silly." His voice was husky.

Leaning down, he flicked his tongue along her neck and down to her breasts. "But you are definitely a feast."

His mouth nibbled her stomach. His tongue snuck into her navel.

The wetness thrilled her.

He drew back, his eyes blazing. "I really was jealous, you know. Of Giovanni's eyes on you. Of the thoughts running through his mind, thoughts identical to mine."

His words thrilled her.

"I wanted you to be only with me." He undid the towel around his waist, raised off her to pull it off, and flung it onto the floor before resuming his position.

His cock stroked her stomach.

She pulled on the ropes.

"Did I make your first time memorable?"

"Yes. So much so that . . . my first time is going to be my last time." Her attempt to sound playful failed.

"This is the last time?" Tension threaded his voice.

"My last time at The Perfect Match."

Tony smiled and resumed his teasing. He moved his hips down, letting his cock rest against her cleft. "I like that answer because I'd like to see you again. When we get home. Not as a Perfect Date."

He put his cock near the entrance to her pussy.

She jutted her hips.

He laughed.

Before she surrendered to his pull, begged for her release, there was one question she had to ask. "Why did you hire a date, when you could've had any woman you wanted?"

Tony stilled. "Because an escort is bound by a confidentiality agreement. Unlike a 'real date'—like the last woman, who talked to an online columnist."

Alyssa tensed and her arousal evaporated. He was talking about Chantelle. He was talking about her. He was talking about her article, "Chantelle Dubois Flies to France for a Yummy Dessert."

"Relax," whispered Tony. He pressed a fingertip against her lips. "No more questions. No more talking. Only feeling."

And as Tony tasted her breasts, words fled from her mind. As he gripped her hips, she forgot how to talk. As he thrust his cock inside of her, she felt only him. His touch, his body.

She thrust her hips, meeting him stroke for stroke.

She yanked on the ropes, straining to get closer, desperate to feel more of him.

He gave and withheld, entered her and withdrew.

Mindless gibberish flew from her lips.

Guttural grunts rumbled in his throat.

As her need merged with his, as her soul sought his, as her orgasm mated with his, her passion washed away the discomfort created by his words.

8

Alyssa gripped the railing as she walked down the stairs in her three-inch heels. Thank God today was the last day of this charade. Either her mind or her neck was going to snap.

She breathed a sigh of relief as she reached the bottom of the stairs. Only twenty more steps to the dining room and then she could hang onto Tony's arm, thereby increasing her odds of making it home alive.

Home.

Tony had said he wanted to see her once they were back home, back to their real lives. A real date, he'd said. One that involved the use of her brain and flat-heeled shoes and a baseball cap, after which they'd engage in a round of bedroom gymnastics, her being a "gymnast" and all.

She smiled.

Now there was an outing to make the God-awful jiggle she had to put into her Ditzy Girl step real. Her mind zipped back to their recent sex and her face warmed. She never would've guessed that she'd like being trussed and tied, that giving into the feeling of being powerless could heighten her orgasm.

She now knew firsthand what Tony must've experienced in the pool, why his climax had been so fast.

Pushing thoughts of sex from her mind, she sighed. One more act and she was through. After adjusting her dress for the tenth useless time, she peeked into the dining room. A buffet was spread out on the side table but no one was there.

She frowned.

Tony had said 11:30, but maybe his meeting with Giovanni was running late.

Great. That meant she'd have to go to the office, which meant thirty more steps. Maybe she should just take off the damn shoes.

No. It was too much work getting them back on. Taking a deep breath and using the wall for support, she made her way down the hall, careful not to get her toothpick heels caught in the plush carpet.

Outside of the door to Giovanni's office, she paused and peeked inside. The two men were at Giovanni's desk, staring at his computer screen.

Plastering a big smile on her face, Alyssa knocked and pushed the door open. "Heeellllooooo," she said in a singsong voice.

Which would have been the perfect greeting had the two men been in a singsong mood. Instead, two hostile faces turned her way. Giovanni looked like he'd just found out he had to climb onto a Stairmaster and lose fifty pounds by the end of the day and Tony . . .

Her smile slipped.

Tony looked like he wished he'd used that rope on her neck instead of her hands.

"Uh . . . did somebody break a fingernail?" She asked in her best girlish voice. Gotta hand it to her. She wasn't one to let a little tension yank her out of character.

"Cut the act, Ms. Sex in San Francisco," sneered Giovanni.

The truth, on the other hand, could yank the best actor right out of her role. Her smile evaporated.

"The Internet is a wonderful thing. I searched my name to show Tony a recent article on Strands and your site popped up, which reminded me why your name sounded familiar." Giovanni waved a file folder in her direction. "I got this information from the attorney I'd hired to sue you. He told me your real name: Alyssa James."

"Is your alias Erica Allen?" asked Tony. His voice was cold.

Alyssa's heart sank. Just when things seemed to be going so well . . .

"Yes."

"And you wrote the article on me and Chantelle?"

"Yes."

"Be glad she only speculated about you, Tony. She tried to ruin my reputation by writing drivel about me in that gossipy rag of hers and . . ."

For the first time in nearly twenty-four hours, heat that was not related to sex rushed through her veins. She'd giggled and wiggled, pretended to be the Tin Man's twin sister, endured extreme sexual deprivation and torture, and finally had mind-blowing sex with a man who—up until this morning—had shown promise of sticking around and this . . . this . . . sleazy toad had the nerve to call her blog a "gossipy rag"? And then say she wrote drivel? Why—

"For your information, Mr. Maffucci, I report the facts. And, you, sir—"

She jabbed at him with a fingertip as she marched forward. Unfortunately, she forgot about the stilts attached to her ankles and pitched forward.

She put her hands out to catch her fall.

Tony leapt forward to catch her.

Her head smacked his and her world went black.

9

When Alyssa opened her eyes, the first thing she noticed was the jackhammer drilling inside her skull. The second thing was the huge bump that had sprouted from the center of Tony's forehead.

She ran a hand along her forehead and felt a matching bump, though hers felt more like a horn. Which proved that her spill onto the carpet had not been a dream.

"Are you all right?" Tony asked, concern replacing the anger previously etched on his face.

"Yeah," she said. She looked around, noticing that she was lying on the couch where Tony had tortured her with his cock. She tried to sit up.

As Tony reached out to assist her, she noticed his hand. His knuckles were red and his hand had swollen to three times its normal size.

"Did I cause that?" she asked.

"No. He did."

A movement behind him drew her gaze. Giovanni's face was red and puffy and the handkerchief he held under his nose was spotted with blood.

Giovanni walked over to her. "Now that you're awake . . . I'm sorry." Lips pressed together, back straight, he turned on his heel and exited the room.

Alyssa pinched her arm. It hurt, so that meant she wasn't dreaming. Maybe she'd traveled to a parallel world. She closed her eyes and reopened them.

Nope. Tony was still looking at her wearing a warm expression. Wasn't he pissed at her before she fell?

"What's going on?" she asked.

"You fell."

"Yeah, that I remember. But the world seems to have changed a lot since then."

Tony shrugged. "Giovanni called you a sneaky, conniving bitch so I slugged him and told him to apologize."

"And he agreed to apologize, just like that?"

"Uh. He needed a bit more persuading."

She raised a brow.

Tony grinned. "I reasoned with him. I said, 'Giovanni, since you *are* the King of Sleaze and the IRS *did* cite you for income tax evasion, how was Alyssa's article, *IRS Out to Dethrone the King of Sleaze,* detrimental to your reputation?'"

Alyssa snorted. "And when that didn't work?"

Tony's grin widened. "I told him that information about some of his more nefarious dealings would mysteriously appear in your e-mail inbox if he didn't apologize."

Smiling, Alyssa nodded. "Ahhh. That makes more sense. And explains why his apology was so heartfelt."

Tony chuckled.

Alyssa's smile faded.

"Guess I ruined your deal. I'm sorry."

"No, you didn't. I called it off—before I punched him."

Alyssa's mouth dropped open. "You did? Why?"

"I didn't want to do business with a man who talked that way about my date."

You called off a business deal for an emotional reason? For me? Though it warmed her heart, she kept those realizations to herself, saying instead, "But you were mad at me, too. Was it because of the story about Chantelle?"

"No. Despite your humorous, sometimes sarcastic tone, I don't find your blog gossipy."

Alyssa felt her head begin to swell with pride.

"In fact, since I didn't even realize Chantelle had started that rumor about us eloping, I found the article informative. I'm going to have to bookmark your site."

Alyssa smiled. "Thank you."

"You're welcome." He leaned forward and kissed her. As usual, the minute his lips touched hers, major endorphin overload kicked in and all rational thought fled her brain, turning her into one big nerve.

Tony broke the kiss, his eyes looking as glazed as she felt. "Hmmm . . . where was I? Oh yes, why I was mad."

Good thing one of them remembered.

"Because I thought you were playing me, just going out with me to get a story about me hiring a date. But, while you were out, Shannon set me straight."

Alyssa frowned. "You called Shannon to ask her

the truth?"

Tony chuckled. "I didn't call Shannon to *ask* her anything. I called her to *accuse* her. I thought she was in on it with you. She explained how you ended up as my date and how you'd promised not to write about me."

"So . . . If I hadn't knocked myself out and I'd told you—instead of Shannon—that I didn't agree to be your date to write about you, would you have believed me?"

"Well, I . . ." He paused and tried again. "I think if you . . ." And again. "Maybe if . . ."

Alyssa narrowed her eyes. "Shall I take that as a 'no'?"

Tony sighed. "Alyssa, I'll be honest. I don't know."

She pretended like the answer didn't hurt. "Why would you believe Shannon?"

"Because, as she said, what would she have to gain by conspiring with you to write about me? It'd only jeopardize her business."

"Whereas, in my business, I'd have everything to gain." Alyssa laughed humorlessly. "Business is business, right?"

Tony frowned. "You already wrote about me once, Alyssa. Isn't it logical for me to think that you'd try to use this situation to write about me again?"

Leave it to a man to use logic.

"Yeah, I guess so—maybe if you'd found out when we first got here. But, I can't believe you'd think that of me after we . . ." *made love* ". . . had sex."

Tony remained silent.

Alyssa sighed.

How could she feel on the cusp of falling into

emotional splendor one second and then feel pushed into an emotional abyss the next? "Well, I guess I won't be calling *The Sin Club* about you," she muttered.

"What? You were going to call into that program and tell the nation I hired a date?"

Alyssa shook her head at Tony's incredulous tone, and stood, shaking off his assistance. "Forget it, Tony. I'm going home."

10

The next day, Alyssa marched into Shannon's office and stalked to her desk.

Shannon looked up and grinned. "I heard—"

"I'm not interested in what you heard. I only agreed to see you in order to collect on my debt." Alyssa paused in front of Shannon and held out her hand.

Shannon frowned. "You'll get payment for the date in thirty days." Her expression changed to one of concern. "Are you experiencing a bit of financial woe?"

"Any woe I'm feeling is all your fault—and it's not financial."

"My fault?"

Alyssa snorted in exasperation and snapped her fingers. "Quit stalling. Pay up."

"Alyssa, I have no idea what you're talking about."

"You said you'd pay me if I propositioned someone. Well, I propositioned Tony and I want my money."

Shannon took Alyssa's hand and put it in the air, high-fiving her. "Way to go! When did you do it? Wait a minute, aren't you mad at Tony?"

"Yes, I am mad at Tony but I did it before then."

"Well, when are you going to do *it?*"

Alyssa stepped back and sank into the lime green chair. Instantly deflated, she sighed—loudly—in defeat. "I already did *it*. Yesterday."

"You broke the contract?"

"Don't screech, Shannon. It's unprofessional."

"Alyssa, I could get my business license revoked. The state—"

Alyssa waved a hand. "Yes, yes, I know. Your words rang in my ears day and night. I had to give in just to get them to stop."

"Oh, no, this is not my fault. You promised."

"Did you really think I could stick to that? Could you? I tried!"

Shannon stared into space, her eyes glazed with worry. "This is bad."

"Don't worry. Tony promised not to tell anyone."

Shannon's gaze snapped to hers. Her lips twisted. "They all promise that."

"What? You mean this happens often?"

Shannon leaned back in her chair and closed her eyes. "Yes. Why do you think I have the contract? Why do you think I stress it over and over again?"

Alyssa's mouth dropped open. "I can't believe you made me feel so guilty, like I'd be betraying our friendship, risking your livelihood—"

"You have risked my livelihood. He still might report me to the state, since you're mad at him! Alyssa, can't you make nice—"

Exasperation instantly reappeared. "Oh, for

71

heaven's sake, he's not—" She paused and narrowed her eyes. "Wait a minute, how did you know that I'm mad at him?"

At that moment, Shannon's phone buzzed. She answered it. "Please send him in, Charlotte." Shannon rose to her feet.

An awful dose of *deja vu* prickled Alyssa. "Shannon—"

Shannon beamed, looking at a spot past Alyssa's left ear. "Tony, what a pleasant surprise."

Oh, so now it's Tony? Alyssa glared at Shannon before turning around.

Her glare dissolved. Oxygen was sucked from her lungs. Anger evaporated from her mind and lust blossomed in her groin.

Tony sauntered into the room, his long legs encased in worn jeans, his buff chest decorated with a snug fitting T-shirt. His satiny hair was loose and tucked behind one ear. His eyes glimmered, his smile dazzled.

He looked boyish and playful and delicious.

"Thanks for your help, Shannon."

"No problem. Well, I'm sure you two have a lot to discuss." She walked from behind the desk and headed toward the door.

Alyssa attempted to summon her anger. "No, we don't."

They both ignored her. Shannon closed the door softly behind her. Tony stopped in front of her.

"I have something for you." He said, removing his iPod and portable headphones from his pocket.

"Oh, you shouldn't have," she squealed, doing her best Lissy impersonation. "Diamonds disguised as a used iPod."

"Alyssa, please listen." He held them out to her.

With a long-suffering sigh, Alyssa slipped the ear pieces into her ears.

Tony pressed play.

Dr. Love filled her head. ". . . so we're going to do things a bit differently with our next caller. I'm going to let him sin on the air. Tony, you're on."

"Thanks, Tom—er, Dr. Love," said Tony.

Alyssa looked at Tony. "You?" she breathed.

"Me," said the real-life Tony.

Alyssa turned her attention back to the recorded Tony.

"I'm a private person so this is a bit rough . . ." His voice had a quaver Alyssa had never heard.

"Take your time, Tony."

"Well . . . my life was ruled by business decisions but then I met Alyssa and, well, she taught me that sometimes you need to make emotional decisions. Like, not to purchase a profitable business from a person you despise, who insults someone you. . . care about and, well, most importantly to believe in someone because your gut—not your mind—tells you they're telling the truth. So. That's my sin— allowing emotion—in the form of Alyssa—into my life. And I hope she'll take me . . ."

A lump grew in Alyssa's throat. Tony, the mystery man who kept his personal life private, had admitted to all that on the air. For her. To convince her.

Alyssa whipped the earphones out of her ears. She threw herself into Tony's arms and hugged him and kissed him and punched him.

"I'll take you," she said softly, smiling up at him.

"Good," said Tony. "Seal it with a kiss."

And she did.

ABOUT THE AUTHOR

Rachelle Chase is an award-winning romance author, business consultant, speaker, and model who's appeared on national television—CBS, as well as "The Morning Show with Mike and Juliet"—plus national radio shows, including "Playboy Radio," the "Hip-Hop Connection," and the "Jordan Rich Show."

An excerpt from "Out of Control," a novella in SECRETS VOLUME 13, was used in ON WRITING ROMANCE, published by Writer's Digest Books, to illustrate how to effectively heighten sexual tension in a romance book.

Published works include:

KICKING THE BUCKET LIST (memoir)
—available 2015
A SINFUL FIANCÉ (The Sin Club Book 4)
—available Spring 2015
HOT DREAMS—available Summer 2015
"The Firefighter Wears Prada" in MEN ON FIRE
SEX LOUNGE
A SINFUL STRIPTEASE (Sin Club Book 1)
A SINFUL PHONE CALL (Sin Club Book 2)
A SINFUL PROPOSITION (Sin Club Book 3)
"Out of Control" in SECRETS VOLUME 13

Read more and sign up for her newsletter at
www.RachelleChase.com.

Here's a hot sneak peek at Rachelle Chase's

SEX LOUNGE

available now . . .

1

Fingertips slipped under her skirt, skimming her thighs.

Nichole gasped and stumbled backward, the book slipping through her fingers as she fell off the stepstool.

Strong hands gripped her hips, righting her.

Taking a deep breath, she opened her mouth to scream, and . . .

Stopped.

That scent. A blend of sandalwood, cloves, leather, and . . . man. Only one man.

Her scream became a whimper.

"Shhhhh . . . " Derek whispered against her neck. A shiver rippled through her.

Thumbs hooked into the waistband of her Nina Ricci thong, sliding it down over her hips.

"What—"

"You know 'what.'"

Hands gripped her hips, pulling her back. Rigid muscle nuzzled her ass.

She moaned.

"Shhhhh . . . "

She was trying to remain quiet. But after enduring months of teasing, months of taunting . . .

"Oh, Derek . . . please." *Nichole groaned and reached behind her. Frantic, needing, wanting . . . NOW.*

Here. In the library. In—

~~~~

At the sound of a throat being cleared, Nichole Simms jumped and slammed her hand over her notebook.

"Good afternoon, Nichole."

Her startled gaze honed in on the perfectly shaped lips, nestled between a neatly trimmed mustache and goatee.

If I nibbled his lips, would it tickle or scratch? If—

She yanked her gaze to his eyes. "M-Mr. Mitchell. Your appointment's not until one."

"I know." Emerald eyes ensnared hers, stealing her breath, jolting her heart.

He stared.

She blushed.

"I'll . . . see if Richard can meet with you now." The mesh penholder toppled onto her desk as she reached for the phone.

Fingers pressed down on hers, the touch light, the sensation searing. "No."

No . . .?

Nichole raised her eyes, staring at the collar of his shirt, afraid to look higher, for fear that he would read her illicit thoughts in her expression. Not that staring at his collar helped, for the crisp whiteness set off his tawny skin while the red silk tie complemented the navy suit. From the corner of her eye, the broad shoulders, accentuated by the tailored drape of his jacket, beckoned her to inspect, to slip her hands under the silk and touch and stroke and—

She returned her gaze to his.

His eyes glittered.

Her knuckles tingled.

Though he stood perfectly still, power seemed to roll off him in waves, mingling with his body heat, concocting a potion impossible to resist.

Okay. She could handle this, maintain the professional façade she always wore like a shield when Derek Mitchell was in the office. He'd just caught her by surprise, that's all.

Uh-huh. Lurid fantasies in which he'd starred had left her feeling more than surprise. Try hot, bothered, wet—

Her face heated. Sliding her hand from under his, Nichole took a deep breath, imagining the air entering her lungs, entering her bloodstream, and dispersing calmness throughout her body. Erasing the feel of fingers caressing her skin. Sweeping away even more sinful acts not yet written . . . but imagined. Restoring order, normalcy, control.

Breathe in . . . Hold it . . .

Breathe out . . . One more time . . .

That was it. She felt better.

Nichole replaced the pens, careful not to look at him.

"Actually," he said, "I wanted to see you first."

And knocked them over again.

"I see." No, she didn't see. She had no idea what he meant. Oh, she knew what she wished he meant— that he wanted to see the real her; the passionate seductress hiding behind the no-nonsense woman who managed Talentz's established and wanna-be models and actors. Of course, there was no chance of that happening. A sexy, wealthy man like Derek Mitchell didn't really see a woman like her, a woman lacking the practiced persona of a sex kitten. Which is why he'd been perfect for the lead role in her fantasies. Because there, her understated, girl-next-door prettiness made him wild with need. He craved her. Devoured her.

All within the safe realm of fantasy.

She stared at him, her gaze impersonal—or so she hoped.

He stared back at her, his gaze intense, seeming to peel the layers in her mind, delving into the core, and uncovering the luscious fantasies of her being stripped and caressed. Outdoors, indoors. In a forest, in a library—

Nichole's eyes darted to her forgotten notebook. She snapped it closed and stacked a pile of papers, casually placing them on top of it. Pasting a polite smile on her face, she struggled to keep her voice even. "How can I help you, Mr. Mitchell?"

www.ingramcontent.com/pod-product-compliance
Lightning Source LLC
Chambersburg PA
CBHW020638130626
46552CB00003B/1298